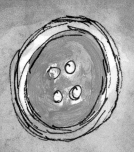

W9-CLQ-475
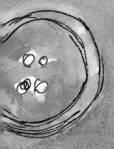
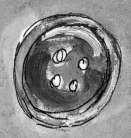
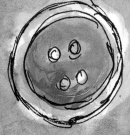

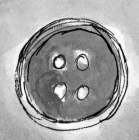

Pete the Cat

and His Four Groovy Buttons

Art by
James Dean
(creator of Pete the Cat)

Story by
Eric Litwin

HARPER
An Imprint of HarperCollinsPublishers

Pete the Cat and His Four Groovy Buttons
Copyright © by James Dean (for the character of Pete the Cat)
Copyright © 2012 by James Dean and Eric Litwin
All rights reserved. Printed in the United States of America.
No part of this book may be used or reproduced in any manner whatsoever without written permission
except in the case of brief quotations embodied in critical articles and reviews.
For information address HarperCollins Children's Books, a division of HarperCollins Publishers,
195 Broadway, New York, NY 10007.
www.harpercollinschildrens.com

Library of Congress Cataloging-in-Publication Data
Litwin, Eric.
    Pete the cat and his four groovy buttons / story by Eric Litwin ; art by James Dean. — 1st ed.
        p.   cm.
    Summary: Pete the cat loves the buttons on his shirt so much that he makes up a song about them, and even as
the buttons pop off, one by one, he still finds a reason to sing.
    ISBN 978-0-06-211058-9 (trade bdg.)
    ISBN 978-0-06-211059-6 (lib. bdg.)
    [1. Cats—Fiction. 2. Buttons—Fiction. 3. Singing—Fiction. 4. Counting.] I. Dean, James, date, ill. II. Title.
PZ7.L7376Pff   2012   2011019366
[E]—dc22   CIP
                                                                                              AC

Typography by Jeanne L. Hogle
14 15 16 17 18 PC 20 19 18 17 16 15 14 13
❖
First Edition

To Trey and Destiny
Always be honest, give more than you take,
and follow your dreams.
—J.D.

To Zelda Litwin, my mother,
whose creative spirit nurtured my imagination.
—E.L.

Pete the Cat put on his favorite shirt with four big, colorful, round, groovy buttons.

He loved his buttons so much, he sang this song:

"My buttons, my buttons,
my four groovy buttons.
My buttons, my buttons,
my four groovy buttons."

OH NO!

One of the buttons popped off
and rolled away.

How many buttons are left?

THREE

3

4 − 1 = 3

Did Pete cry?
Goodness, no!
Buttons come and buttons go.

He kept on singing his song:

"My buttons, my buttons,
my three groovy buttons.
My buttons, my buttons,
my three groovy buttons."

POP!

OH NO!

Another button popped off and rolled away!

How many buttons are left?

TWO

2

3-1=2

Did Pete cry?
Goodness, no!

Buttons come and
buttons go.

He kept on singing his song:

"My buttons, my buttons,
    my two groovy buttons.
My buttons, my buttons,
my two groovy buttons."

POP!

OH NO!

Another button popped off and rolled away!

How many buttons are left?

ONE

1

2 - 1 = 1

Did Pete cry?
Goodness, no!

Buttons come and buttons go.

He kept on singing his song:

"My button, my button,
my one groovy button.
My button, my button,
my one groovy button."

The last button popped off and rolled away!

How many buttons are left?

ZERO

1-1=0

Did Pete cry?
Goodness, no!

Buttons come and buttons go.

Pete looked down at his buttonless shirt,
and what do you think he saw?

HIS BELLY BUTTON!

And he kept on singing his song:

"My button, my button,
still have my belly button.
My button, my button,
still have my belly button."

I guess it simply goes to show that stuff will come and stuff will go.

But do we cry?

Goodness, NO!

We keep on singing.

Buttons come and buttons go.

J PICTURE LITWIN

Litwin, Eric.
Pete the cat and his
four groovy buttons

NWEST

R4000348050

NORTHWEST
Atlanta-Fulton Public Library